◆ ◆ ◆ CHARLOTTE HERMAN

MAX MALONE
Makes a Million

◆ Illustrated by
Cat Bowman Smith

Henry Holt and Company ◆ New York

With love to Hillel, dearer than any million　—C.H.

To my first friends, Evelyn and George　—C.B.S.

Henry Holt and Company, LLC
Publishers since 1866
115 West 18th Street
New York, New York 10011

Henry Holt is a registered trademark of Henry Holt and Company, LLC
Text copyright © 1991 by Charlotte Herman
Illustrations copyright © 1991 by Catherine Bowman Smith
All rights reserved.
Distributed in Canada by H. B. Fenn and Company Ltd.

Library of Congress Cataloging-in-Publication Data
Herman, Charlotte.
Max Malone makes a million / Charlotte Herman; illustrated by Cat Bowman Smith (Redfeather Books).
Summary: Max Malone, along with his best friend, Gordy, is continually frustrated in his attempts to get rich, while his neighbor, little Austin Healy, makes money at every turn.
[1. Moneymaking projects—Fiction.] I. Smith, Cat Bowman, ill. II. Title. III. Series.
PZ7.H4313Mc 1991 [E]—dc20 90-46373

ISBN 0-8050-1374-1 (hardcover)
10　9　8　7　6　5　4　3
ISBN 0-8050-2328-3 (paperback)
20　19　18

Published in hardcover in 1991 by Henry Holt and Company
First Redfeather paperback edition—1992
Printed in Mexico

Contents

In the Chips

Max Malone was lying on the living-room floor. He was reading the Sunday comics and laughing at the latest adventures of Garfield.

His sister Rosalie was working on a crossword puzzle at the dining-room table. "Does anyone know a five-letter word that ends in *t* and means 'silent'?"

"Quiet!" Max ordered. "I'm trying to read."

" 'Quiet'! That's it! Thanks, Max."

Mrs. Malone was on the couch, reading the other parts of the paper. She especially liked the human-interest stories. Those were the stories about dogs who saved entire families from burning buildings. Or firemen who rescued cats from trees.

"Now, this is interesting," said Mrs. Malone. "A ten-year-old boy made a fortune selling chocolate-chip cookies."

Max looked up from the comics and listened as his mother read:

> "TEN-YEAR-OLD IN THE CHIPS
> "Ten-year-old Anthony Baker of Portland, Oregon, doesn't have to steal cookies from the cookie jar. He puts them there. And judging by the number of cookies he's baked using his own original recipe, he's been filling lots of cookie jars.
> "Anthony doesn't know exactly how many cookies he's baked so far. He's not counting. He's too busy counting the money he's making."

"Let me see that," said Max, jumping to his feet. He hurried over to the couch and sat down next to his mother. She handed him the paper, and he began reading silently. He interrupted himself with lots of "Wow"s and "Oh, boy"s.

"Wow! All he did was buy an old stove. And he rented an old shack in his neighborhood, where he baked and sold the cookies." Max continued to read to himself, until he came to the last line. "Oh, boy, listen to what it says here: 'This young man may well be on his way to becoming a millionaire.' "

Max tossed the newspaper onto the couch. "Wow! A millionaire, just by baking and selling chocolate-chip cookies. I could do that." He had watched his mother bake cookies lots of times. There was nothing to it. "I could get an old stove and rent a shack somewhere."

"There aren't any shacks around here," Rosalie informed him.

Max thought this over. Rosalie was right. He couldn't remember seeing any shacks in his neighborhood.

"Then I'll just use our kitchen. We've got an old stove." He ran into the kitchen to check out the stove. Rosalie followed him. Max opened and closed the oven door and worked the control knob a couple of times. "This stove should work out even better. I already know how to use it. All I have to do is get Gordy to help me."

"I'll help you too," said Rosalie. "You'll need all the help you can get."

That's just what Max didn't need. Rosalie's help. She loved to eat anything that was sweet. She could eat tons of sugared cereal and never get tired of it. He could just imagine what she'd do with his cookies.

"No thanks," said Max. "You'd eat them faster than we could bake them."

"I'm not sure about this cookie business of yours," said Mrs. Malone, coming into the kitchen to pour herself a cup of coffee. "I don't like the idea of your fooling around with the stove. And the mess . . ."

"Come on, Mom. What if Anthony Baker's mother told him not to fool around with the stove and worried about making a mess? He never would've made his fortune."

Mrs. Malone leaned against the counter, took a sip of coffee, and sighed deeply. "Oh, well. I guess I ought to let you give it a try. Twenty years from now I don't want you to come to me and tell me that I kept you from becoming a millionaire. Just be careful."

With an air of victory, Max raised his arms and shook his fists, the way he had seen athletes in the Olympics do. "All riiiight! Just you wait and see, Mom. We'll make so much money, you won't have to sell any more memo pads." Mrs. Malone sold personalized memo pads through the mail.

"I'd better go call Gordy," said Max, running to the phone.

Max punched in Gordy's number and waited for someone to answer. He hoped it wouldn't be Gordy's mother or father. He hated talking to parents on the phone and having to be polite.

Luckily it was Gordy who finally answered, and Max didn't waste any time on small talk. He got straight to the point.

"Gordy, get over here right away. You, pal, are about to make your fortune!"

Quality Ingredients

"**E**ggs," Gordy called out.

"Check," answered Max.

"Flour."

"Check."

"Sugar."

"Check."

Gordy continued to read off the list of ingredients on the back of the package of chocolate chips, while Max checked to see what was in stock in his kitchen.

"Baking soda," Gordy read on.

"No baking soda," said Max. "But we've got baking powder."

"Good enough," said Gordy. "Okay, that's everything on the list. We're all set." Gordy was just as excited as Max was about making a million dollars, and was anxious to start their business. He had wasted no time in getting over to Max's house.

"Then let's do it," said Max as he preheated the oven to 375°, the way his mother always did when she baked cookies.

"Hey, wait a minute," interrupted Rosalie, who had been standing by watching and hoping to be asked for help. "You can't use that recipe. What's the point? Anyone can bake those cookies. You need an original recipe. Like Anthony Baker had."

Max tucked his chin in the space between his thumb and index finger and did some heavy thinking.

"Rosalie is right," he said finally. "We've got to

change the recipe by adding some other ingredients too."

"May I make a suggestion?" asked Mrs. Malone, who had gotten off the phone just in time to hear that last remark. "First bake the cookies using the recipe on the back of the package. Then once you get it perfect, you can vary it here and there and do a little experimenting."

"That'll take too much time," said Max. "We want to get started on the baking right away." He took out two bowls, measuring cups and spoons, and his mother's electric hand mixer.

While Gordy began combining the flour, baking powder, and salt in one bowl, Max measured the white and brown sugars, butter, and vanilla into the other.

"Oops!" said Gordy. "I seem to have lost some flour."

Max looked up from his bowl to see Gordy enveloped in a cloud of all-purpose flour. He also noticed

that there was more flour on the counter and on the floor than there was in the bowl.

"That's okay," said Max. "Just add some more."

"I don't know how much I spilled."

"Guess," said Max. "What's the difference? It's an original recipe anyway."

"I think I'd better leave," said Mrs. Malone, touching her hand to her forehead and hurrying out of the kitchen.

"What now?" asked Gordy.

"It's time to add our original ingredients," said Max. He opened up the refrigerator and discovered a jar of honey. He held it up for Gordy to see. "Like honey, for instance."

"Honey is good," said Gordy. "It's a quality ingredient. My father says we should use only quality ingredients in our cookies. People appreciate quality in a product and won't settle for less."

"Yogurt is quality," came a voice that could no longer keep quiet. From where she was sitting, on a stool in a corner of the kitchen, Rosalie began to throw out suggestions. "Cinnamon is quality. So are nutmeg, and cloves, and ginger."

"I was getting to that," said Max.

"And add more brown sugar. It'll give the cookies a rich, golden appearance."

Max added cinnamon, nutmeg, cloves, ginger, and an extra cup of brown sugar. "I think that's enough original ingredients." He picked up the mixer, positioned the beaters in the bowl and pushed the switch to low.

"Hey," Max called above the noise of the mixer. "There's something wrong here. It's not beating right."

"You forgot the eggs," Rosalie shouted to him.

"Oh, right." Max turned off the mixer and added two eggs according to the recipe, and one more because of all the extra ingredients. He started up the mixer again on high.

All the quality ingredients shot up in the air and

splattered all over the counter and all over Max. He set the speed to medium and tried again. Everything blended together smoothly. He gradually added Gordy's flour mixture.

"This is easy enough," said Max as he and Gordy dropped spoonfuls of the mixture onto two ungreased cookie sheets. They placed the cookies in the oven and peered through the window of the oven door to watch them bake. Rosalie licked the batter from the bowl.

"Oops," said Gordy. "I think there is something seriously wrong with these chocolate-chip cookies."

"What?" asked Max.

"We forgot the chocolate chips."

Max slapped his forehead. "I can't believe it. We forgot the most important ingredient."

"Oh, well," said Gordy. "This will be our practice batch."

Rosalie pushed Max and Gordy aside so she could

look through the window. "I think you'll need lots of practice. The cookies aren't rising. They're flat. Like pancakes."

"Two very large pancakes," said Max, as he watched the batter run together.

When the cookie-pancakes began turning brown around the edges, Max took the cookie sheets out of the oven. "We'd better try again. Only this time we'll double the recipe. And we'll use the recipe on the back of the package. We've wasted too much time already."

While Rosalie was nibbling on the practice cookies, Max and Gordy combined all the ingredients in two larger bowls. This time they remembered to add the chocolate chips.

They took out extra baking pans from the cabinet and dropped spoonfuls of batter onto them. "These should work," said Max, placing the pans in the oven. "Now let's figure out how much to sell them for." He took a pencil from the drawer, and a pad of paper that said *From the desk of* MAX MALONE. Then he and Gordy sat down at the kitchen table.

"All right," said Max, as he doodled on the pad. "How should we sell them? By the cookie or by the pound?"

"The shop in the mall sells them by the pound," Rosalie offered. "Mmm. Semi-sweet chocolate chips with macadamia nuts. I can taste them now."

"I like the white chocolate with macadamia nuts," said Gordy.

"Come on, you guys," said Max. "You're wasting time."

The doorbell rang. It was Austin Healy, from across the street. He was just six years old, and didn't even care that his father had named him after a car.

"Something smells good in here," said Austin, sniffing the air.

"It's our cookies," said Max. "We're going into the cookie business. We're going to make a million."

"Can I go into business with you?" Austin asked. "I'd like to make a million too."

"You're too young," said Max. "This is a real business. We're not just playing. Maybe when you're older."

"Are you going into the pancake business too?" Austin asked, glancing at Rosalie, who was eating the cookie-pancakes.

"Oh, that," said Max. "That was just our practice batch."

"I think you've got two practice batches," said Rosalie. "Your cookies are burning."

Max and Gordy made a dash for the oven. "Oh, no!" said Max as he began taking out the pans. "They're ruined."

Instead of being golden brown, the cookies were a very dark brown with black around the edges.

"I guess you'll have to try again," said Austin.

"We've already tried twice," said Gordy. "I don't think I can handle a third time."

"We're all out of ingredients anyway," said Max. He slumped into his chair. He wondered if Anthony Baker had had all this trouble.

"I think," said Austin as he helped himself to a piece of Rosalie's cookie-pancakes, "I think you should go into another business. Do something you know how to do." He helped himself to a second piece and walked out the door.

Big Business

"**W**hat do we know how to do?" Gordy asked Max.

"Nothing," Max answered.

They were resting on Max's front steps after cleaning up Mrs. Malone's kitchen. Max was trying to figure out where he had gone wrong, and where Anthony Baker had gone right. Maybe Anthony had an older stove. Or a better recipe.

"We'd better think of something fast," said Gordy. "Vacation is over in two weeks."

Max sighed deeply. Then he shut his eyes and tried to think of something he knew how to do.

Something he knew about. He knew about garage sales. One of his favorite things to do was to buy lots of great junk at Mrs. Filbert's garage sales. Mrs. Filbert was Max's neighbor. Max and Gordy could have a garage sale. The problem was, Max didn't have a garage. Neither did Gordy.

The door swung open and out came Mrs. Malone with two glasses of lemonade. "Here, boys. I think you can use this."

"Hey, thanks," said Max and Gordy, taking the glasses from her. They gulped down their drinks.

"Boy, this lemonade hits the spot," said Gordy.

"Lemonade!" shouted Max, jumping to his feet. "That's it. We'll make our millions in lemonade."

"Are you kidding? We tried to sell the stuff lots of times. Rosalie drank most of it. She charged it and never paid us back. We didn't make a single penny."

"We weren't running a real business before," said Max. "We were just fooling around. Besides, do you have any better ideas?"

"No," answered Gordy.

"Then we'll sell lemonade," said Max. "It's easy to make. And it's cheap." He could just picture it. First they would sell lemonade from a stand. And when they became real successful, they would go on to big business. They could sell frozen lemonade in a supermarket. Or fresh, in cartons.

The next day Max and Gordy set up their lemonade stand in the park. Max had a pitcher filled with lemonade made from fresh lemons. He had added sugar little by little, until he got it to taste just right. He topped it all off with ice cubes. Gordy brought a small folding table, two chairs, and paper cups. They hung a sign from the table. It read:

LEMONADE

25 cents

"Business should be real good," said Max. "It's going to be a hot day."

They sat down at the table. They tried to look very businesslike while they waited for their first customer.

Soon their first customer was walking toward them. It was Rosalie.

"I'd like to try some of your lemonade," she said.

"That will be twenty-five cents," said Max.

"Charge it," said Rosalie.

"Cash only," said Max.

Rosalie hesitated for a moment. Then she dug into her pocket and came up with a quarter. She plunked it down on the table. Max and Gordy exchanged smiles. They were proud of how businesslike they were acting. Max poured some lemonade into a cup and watched her drink it.

"Just as I thought," she said. "It isn't sweet enough." She turned to leave. "Maybe I'll bring you some more sugar later."

What Max and Gordy needed were more

customers. At this rate Max's mother would be selling memo pads forever. "The park is so empty today," said Max.

"Probably because of the heat," said Gordy.

"I sure am thirsty," said Max.

"Me too," said Gordy.

"I've been thinking," said Max. "Maybe we should taste the lemonade again. To see if Rosalie is right about the sugar."

"Good idea," said Gordy. "We don't want to sell sour lemonade."

Each poured himself a cup and drank it down in one gulp.

"It's sweet enough for me," said Max.

"Plenty sweet," said Gordy. "Let's try a little more. Just to be sure."

After the second cup, they waited for more customers. The sun was beating down on them. The ice cubes were beginning to melt. They poured themselves some more lemonade.

"It's only right that we taste it again," said Max. "To see if melted ice cubes affect the flavor."

They drank the lemonade and decided that it was still sweet enough. Then they waited some more.

Finally three small boys followed by their mother ran into the park.

"At last," said Max.

"This is it," said Gordy.

"Hey, lemonade!" the oldest boy shouted.

"Yay, lemonade!" shouted the younger ones. And all three ran toward Max and Gordy.

"An easy seventy-five cents," said Max.

"Maybe even a dollar," said Gordy when he saw the mother coming after her sons.

"We want lemonade," the boys told their mother.

"Not now," she said.

"But we're thirsty."

"We don't know what's in it," she whispered as she led them away.

Max and Gordy were angry. And insulted.

"What does she think is in here, anyway?" asked Max.

"Yeah," said Gordy. "Poison?"

They poured themselves some more lemonade and drank it. They wanted the mother to see them drinking it. She would see that it wasn't poisoned. Besides, they were thirsty. And hot. The ice cubes had melted completely.

"This tastes like sour water," said Max.

"Yeah," said Gordy. "Warm sour water. It's definitely not quality."

"It needs more sugar," said Max.

By the time Rosalie came back with some sugar, Max and Gordy were ready to leave.

"How was business?" asked Rosalie.

"Slow," said Max.

"Too bad," said Rosalie. "Austin is making a fortune."

"Austin is selling lemonade?" asked Max.

"Yes. Two kinds. One made with sugar, and one with Sweet 'n Low. Remember when we saw those men chopping up that sidewalk on Friday?" She began adding sugar to the lemonade.

"Yeah," said Max. "In front of the post office."

"Well, today they're pouring cement for the new sidewalk. And that's where Austin is." She sat down at the table and little by little drank up the rest of the lemonade.

They took apart the stand and dropped everything off at Max's house. Then they hurried over to the post office.

Sure enough, there was Austin selling lemonade to three construction workers, who were standing in line. Two ladies coming out of the post office stood behind them to buy lemonade from "that cute little boy."

Max and Gordy exchanged angry glances. This was definitely not fair. Making a million dollars was Max's idea. Not Austin's.

"Hi, guys," Austin called when his customers left. "Want a drink?"

"We're not thirsty," said Max. He could still taste the warm lemonade, which was starting to rise up to his throat. He probably wouldn't touch the stuff for the rest of the summer.

"How's business?" asked Max. He knew the answer even before Austin gave it.

"It's great. I figured I'd get some practice on my own before I'm old enough to join up with you." He poured himself a cup of water and drank it down.

"What's the matter, Austin?" asked Gordy. "Don't you trust your lemonade?"

"I don't want to drink up all my profits," Austin answered. "When I'm thirsty, I drink the water. And I sell the lemonade."

Max watched the people walking in and out of the post office. He watched the construction workers wiping sweat off their faces. So many people. So many *thirsty* people. Why hadn't he thought to come here?

"You picked a pretty good spot to set up your stand," said Max. He hated to admit it, but it was true.

"Yeah," said Austin. "I knew these men would be here today. I knew they'd be thirsty. You just have to be in the right place at the right time. You've got to know your market. Know your customers. Too bad they won't be here tomorrow. I'll have to figure out something else to do."

Max watched Austin empty the cup of money into his pockets. He could see the quarters, nickels, and dimes pouring out of the cup. He even saw a dollar bill.

"Boy. Making a million dollars sure is fun," said Austin. "I can't wait until tomorrow."

♦ ♦ ♦ ♦ ♦ ♦ ♦ ♦ ♦ ♦ ♦ ♦ ♦ ♦ ♦ *4*

What Next?

Max couldn't wait until tomorrow either. He woke up early in the morning to spy on Austin. He wanted to see how Austin was going to make the rest of his million.

Probably nothing would happen. Yesterday was just a fluke. A lucky break. What would a little kid like Austin know about making money, anyway? But Max had to be ready. Just in case.

He sat on his front steps, spying on Austin's house and pretending to be reading a newspaper. Detectives in movies always did that sort of thing.

Only they usually leaned against lampposts or sat on benches while they spied.

The newspaper Max was using was the old Sunday paper. The one that told about Anthony Baker. He had been saving it. But later, after he finished spying, he would throw it away. He didn't want to be reminded of Anthony Baker's success in the cookie business.

Max peered over the top of the paper. Nothing was happening in front of Austin's house. The shades were down. Austin was probably still asleep. Max's eyes were growing tired of peering. His arms were becoming tired from holding up the paper in front of his face. Just when Max was about to go back to bed, Gordy came by with a pair of binoculars.

"I thought this might help," he said, sitting down next to Max.

"Won't Austin think it's suspicious if we stare at him through binoculars?" Max asked.

"We can always tell him we're bird watching," Gordy answered.

They took turns using the binoculars. At last Austin came out of the house, holding a small bag.

"There he is," announced Max, whose turn it was to use the binoculars.

"I see him," said Gordy. "He's going next door. He's knocking."

Max took the binoculars away from his eyes. He could see better without them. He could see the lady who opened the door. She and Austin began talking. Austin took something out of the bag and showed it to her. The lady smiled.

"What's he showing her?" Gordy asked. He grabbed the binoculars from Max and looked through them. "I can't see what it is."

The lady disappeared from the doorway, then came back again. She handed something to Austin.

"Money," said Max. "She's giving him money. She's buying something from him."

After that house Austin went on to the next one. The same thing happened there. Austin sold, and someone bought. It happened at the third house too.

Max and Gordy crossed the street and began following him. At almost every house somebody bought something from Austin Healy. But what were they buying?

When Austin was finished with the last house on his side of the street, he crossed over and started on the other side. Max's side. Max and Gordy hid behind some bushes and watched. Austin went from house to house. One house that he went to was very familiar.

"Hey!" cried Max. "That's my house."

Austin knocked on the door. A familiar lady answered.

"And that's your mother," said Gordy.

Max couldn't believe his eyes. His mother took what Austin was showing her. Then she reached into the pocket of her jeans and handed him some money.

"I can't believe my eyes," said Max. "My own mother. She's actually buying something from that squirt."

Max could hardly wait for Austin to start on the houses around the corner. As soon as the coast was clear, he and Gordy ducked out from behind the bushes. They ran straight to Max's house.

Max confronted his mother in the linen closet. "Okay," he said. "Admit it. You bought something from Austin Healy."

Mrs. Malone threw her hands up in the air. A washcloth was dangling from one of them. "All right. You caught me. I surrender."

"What did you buy from him?" asked Max.

"It's on my desk. Take a look."

Max went into the kitchen. His eyes searched the desk with its stacks of memo pads and order forms. And then he saw it.

"A seashell? You bought a seashell from Austin?"

"It's a conch shell," said Rosalie, who poked her head out from the pantry. Max noticed traces of powdered sugar around her mouth. "We learned about them in science last year."

"Isn't it lovely?" asked Mrs. Malone, coming into the kitchen. "I thought it would be something pretty to look at while I make out my orders. And it was a real bargain. Just twenty-five cents." She picked up the shell and held it to her ear. "It's a small shell, but you can still hear the sound of the sea." She passed the shell around, and everyone took turns listening to the sea.

"I can't think of anyone who doesn't like sea-shells," said Mrs. Malone. And she held it to her ear again.

Back on the steps, Gordy told Max, "My father once gave me a shell like that. He went on vacation to Florida and brought it back from the beach."

Max practically fell off the steps. The beach! Of course. That was it. They could collect those shells at the beach. And as soon as Austin ran out of his supply, Max and Gordy could move in.

"Come on," said Max, slapping Gordy on the back. "We're off to the beach. Our fortune is just a bike ride away."

Searching for Seashells

"**P**ure profit," said Max. "We get the shells for free, and then we sell them."

They were walking their bikes along the shore. And they were barefoot. Gentle waves slapped at their feet and tickled their toes.

"I just wish we would find them already," said Gordy. "All we ever see are pebbles."

"Ouch!" said Max, rubbing his foot. "And some of them are sharp too." Max had been to the beach lots of times. And thinking about it now, he didn't remember ever seeing any seashells. But maybe it was because he hadn't been looking for any.

They walked along the beach, getting splashed by kids who were jumping into the water. They walked around little kids who were digging in the sand. Probably trying to reach China, Max thought. And all that time, Max and Gordy kept their eyes open for seashells. Conchs, like Austin sold. Any kind.

But there were no conchs. There was nothing but pebbles. And tiny pieces of shells that looked like eggshells. Wet and sandy, and with their bike bags empty, Max and Gordy pedaled home.

Rosalie was lying on the grass in front of the house. She was reading *Gone With the Wind*. Max had bought it for her at one of Mrs. Filbert's garage sales.

"You look like drowned rats," she told Max and Gordy when she glanced up from her book.

"We just came from the beach," Max explained. "We were looking for seashells like Austin had. But we couldn't find any."

Rosalie began rolling on the grass and laughing hysterically. "You were looking for conchs in Lake Michigan? I can't believe it." She rolled around some more, and then she sat up. "You can't find those kinds of shells at the lake. You've got to go to the ocean." She started laughing all over again.

That Rosalie. She was always acting like such a know-it-all. When he made his million, he would buy her a house of her own. Then he wouldn't have to live with her.

"Thanks for telling me," said Max. "I'll just go see if I can find an ocean somewhere."

Max and Gordy did not go looking for an ocean. Gordy went home. And later, Max went looking for Austin. He didn't have to look far. He found him sitting on the curb in front of his house, counting money. Real money. Not just nickels, dimes, and quarters. But dollar bills.

"Hey, Austin," said Max. "Where did you get all that money?"

"From the bank," said Austin. "I changed all my coins for dollar bills. The coins were getting too heavy."

"You earned all that money yourself?"

"Sure. Some from the lemonade. And some from the seashells."

"That was a nice shell you sold my mom," Max said. "Did you get it from the ocean?"

"No," said Austin. "From the pet store. That was my source. And I bought in quantity. It's cheaper that way. Thirty shells to a package. I paid two dollars, and I sold each shell for a quarter."

Austin divided his money into two piles. "I'm saving some and spending some," he said, running into his house and back out again. "See you later, Max. I'm going to the pet store."

"For more shells?" Max asked.

"No," said Austin. "I don't need any more. I've already sold to most of the people in the neighborhood. And I'm not allowed to go to strange houses.

Now I'm going to buy something I've always wanted. A red-spotted newt."

Max stood at the curb and watched Austin run down the street. It wasn't fair. First Anthony Baker, and now Austin Healy. Everyone, it seemed, was making money. Everyone except Max Malone.

Backyard Carnival

Rosalie was watching an old movie on TV. It was called *South Pacific,* and she was singing along with the music. She was singing something about washing a man out of her hair. Max shook his head. He couldn't figure out how Rosalie could enjoy old movies so much. She was always watching them. With noise coming from the TV and from Rosalie, Max couldn't hear himself think. And he needed to do some heavy thinking. It had been two days since Austin had made a fortune in seashells. And Max still hadn't come up with a way to make his million.

A commercial came on, and Rosalie stopped singing.

"Oh, that's so romantic," she said, clasping her hands together.

"What? The movie? asked Max.

"No, the commercial. It's for a cruise. The Carnival Cruise."

"Wow! That's great," said Max.

"You're interested in the cruise?" Rosalie asked.

"No. The carnival. I don't know why I didn't think of it before. A backyard carnival is a great way to make money. We'll have food and prizes, and we'll make the games ourselves."

"You need money to start a carnival," said Rosalie. "And you don't have any."

"I'll take out a loan," said Max.

On Friday morning Max and Gordy were on their way to buy food and prizes. Max had convinced his mother to lend him ten dollars. He would pay her back as soon as he made money from the carnival.

Gordy took out a ten-dollar loan from his mother too. First they went looking for food.

"Taffy apples," Max suggested. "That's a good carnival food." He thought that cotton candy was a good carnival food too. But he didn't know how he could make it in his backyard.

"Good idea," said Gordy. "We can buy them cheap at the candy outlet store. No one will mind the broken sticks."

At the store they bought twenty taffy apples for twenty-five cents apiece. "We'll sell them for fifty cents each," said Max. "Double our money. And now for the fun stuff. Let's go get the prizes. We've got fifteen dollars to spend."

"My father said we should try to find quality prizes," said Gordy. "People will be more likely to play the games if they know they can win quality prizes."

"Yeah. None of that junky stuff," said Max as they were walking. "No liquid bubbles, or slime, or things like that. We'll look for Nerf footballs and Teenage Mutant Ninja Turtles. Prizes kids will want to win."

At Toys for Less, Max and Gordy walked up and down the aisles and searched for cheap, quality prizes. They were hard to find. Everything was either junky and cheap, or quality and expensive. After exploring the entire store, they finally decided on yo-yos, kites, Slinkys, and Silly Putty. They were not junky, and they were pretty cheap.

Max and Gordy brought their prizes and taffy apples to Max's house. Then they went into the backyard to plan their carnival.

"We can have them knock over tin cans with a ball," said Max.

"And pitch balls into pails," said Gordy.

"And guess the number of jelly beans in a fish-bowl," said Max. He thought of the two packages of jelly beans Mrs. Malone had bought for Rosalie the other day. Max didn't care much for jelly beans.

They got stuck in his teeth. But Rosalie loved them.

"You should put on a show," said Rosalie, who came over to offer her suggestion. "I can sing for you. I know the entire score of *South Pacific*."

"No thanks," said Max. "We want to attract customers. Not chase them away." He slapped Gordy on the back, and they both burst out laughing. Rosalie walked away in a huff.

Max and Gordy continued planning. Then they found large pieces of cardboard and built their games. On one piece of cardboard they painted a clown's face. They cut a hole in his mouth for a bean-bag toss. On another piece of cardboard they cut a hole large enough for a head to stick through.

"Someone puts his face through the hole," Max explained. "And people throw wet sponges at it."

"Whose face?" Gordy asked. "Not mine."

"Not mine either," said Max. "But don't worry. I'll think of someone."

All day long Max and Gordy cut, drew, pasted, and hammered. They gathered empty Coke cans that Mrs. Malone had been saving for recycling to use for their game. And they filled Max's old fishbowl with Rosalie's jelly beans.

On Saturday, Max and Gordy put up signs all around the neighborhood, announcing their main event on Sunday. And when Sunday arrived, everything was ready.

Kids came from all around. Some even came with their parents. Rosalie was in charge of ticket sales: five for a dollar. The kids knocked over Coke cans. They pitched balls into pails. And they threw wet sponges at Austin Healy's face. Mrs. Malone served iced tea at twenty-five cents a glass. And she sold all the taffy apples. There was only one problem. Max and Gordy were running out of prizes.

"Everyone's winning," said Max.

"We made the games too easy," said Gordy.

Rosalie volunteered to run out and buy more

prizes and taffy apples with the money they were making from the carnival.

A half hour later she was back, eating a taffy apple.

"I'm back," she called to Max. "Just look at all the sensible prizes I bought for you."

Max poked his head into a bag full of liquid bubbles, slime, plastic jewelry, and school supplies.

"You bought school supplies for a carnival?" cried Max. "Who wants to win erasers and pencil sharpeners?"

"They were on sale," said Rosalie. "And besides, school will be starting soon. They're very practical."

Max didn't have time to argue. Too many people were waiting for their prizes.

When all the prizes were gone, Max and Gordy decided that the carnival was over. Everyone went away happy. Especially Austin Healy, who'd won the jelly beans by guessing that there were two

hundred and ten of them in the fishbowl. He'd won the fishbowl too.

"Just look at all this money," said Max after everyone left. "I can't wait to see how much we made." They counted up all the nickels, dimes, quarters, and dollar bills.

"Wow!" said Max. "Twenty-five dollars. We almost made a fortune."

"Not quite," said Gordy, reaching into the pile. "I owe my mother ten dollars."

Max slapped his forehead. "Oh, no. I forgot all about that." He let out a deep sigh and took ten dollars from the pile too. That left them with just five dollars. "Two fifty each," he said. "Bummer. Not much of a fortune, is it?"

"You can say that again," said Gordy.

♦ ♦ ♦ ♦ ♦ ♦ ♦ ♦ ♦ ♦ ♦ ♦ ♦ ♦ ♦**7**

Copycat Austin

*T*he following Sunday there were new signs all around the neighborhood. Someone else was having a carnival that afternoon. Max recognized the address. "Hey, that's Austin Healy's house," he announced to Gordy.

"Copycat," said Gordy. "Just wait until he sees how much work he has to do for five dollars."

At one o'clock Max and Gordy walked over to Austin's house. There were signs on the front lawn:

CARNIVAL
Live Animals!
Live Entertainment!

Max and Gordy could hear voices in the back-yard, and someone singing. The singing grew louder as they entered the yard. A crowd of people surrounded the singer. She was singing something about meeting a stranger across a crowded room.

The song was familiar. So was the voice. It was Rosalie's. And she was singing "Some Enchanted Evening" from *South Pacific.*

When she was finished, everyone applauded. Rosalie took a bow and began another song.

Max couldn't get over it. Rosalie's voice wasn't so bad. Or maybe she just sounded better outside. If he had only known, he would have had live entertainment too.

All around the yard there were tables set up with prizes. Wonderful prizes. Large stuffed animals, just like at real carnivals.

"True quality," said Gordy.

"Hi, guys," said Austin. "I'm glad you could come."

"Boy, you must have spent a fortune on these prizes," Max said happily. He figured that Austin spent so much on prizes that he wouldn't make any money from the carnival.

"I didn't spend anything," said Austin. "I had the prizes donated. I went from house to house, asking people for old stuffed animals they didn't want any more. Mrs. Filbert had the best ones."

Mrs. Filbert was at Austin's carnival too, with her Great Dane, Phyllis. And next to a sign that said DOG SHOW, a group of kids gathered to watch Phyllis sit up and beg, chase her tail, and play dead.

"Is Phyllis your live animal?" asked Max after Gordy ran over to watch Phyllis roll over.

"She's one of them," said Austin. "The other is Newton."

"Newton?" asked Max.

"My red-spotted newt," said Austin. He pointed to a table with a fishbowl on it. In the bowl was Newton. Two small girls were talking and waving to it.

Max looked around Austin's yard. There were more kids here than there had been at Max's carnival. They were eating popcorn and laughing at Phyllis, who was chasing her tail. And they seemed to be enjoying Rosalie's singing. Newton was drawing a large crowd too. Max had to admit that there was a lot going on here. But there was one thing Max had at his carnival that Austin didn't have.

"I see you don't have any taffy apples here," he said.

"There's more profit in popcorn," said Austin. "It's cheap to make, and you can sell it for the same price as taffy apples. And everyone likes popcorn. Especially me. Sometimes I think I like it too much. I've got a little stomachache." He rubbed the side of his stomach. "But I don't care. As long as I feel good by Friday."

"What's on Friday?" asked Max. Probably Austin had another money-making plan. Maybe Max could get in on it this time.

"Dusty Field is signing autographs at the sporting-goods store. I really want to meet him."

Dusty Field was a famous local ball player. He used to live in Max's neighborhood, and now played in the minors. There was talk that he was going up to the majors soon. It would be a great chance to meet him.

"Maybe I'll see you there," said Max.

Some kids standing at a board with a large hole cut into it called for Austin.

"I've got to go," he told Max. "They're waiting to throw wet sponges at me."

As Austin ran off, Max thought of a story he had once read. It was about King Midas. Everything he

touched turned to gold. It was sort of like that with Austin. Everything he did made money for him. Everything always worked out for him. It wasn't fair. Max felt like throwing a wet sponge at Austin's face too.

Instead he watched the other kids do it. And he watched Phyllis roll over and chase her tail. And he listened to Rosalie sing "There Is Nothing Like a Dame." Then he turned around and went home.

Baseballs for Sale

"**A**ustin Healy is having his appendix out today," said Max.

"Yeah, I heard about that," said Gordy. "He threw up all his popcorn last night. Too bad he has to miss Dusty Field on Friday."

Max and Gordy were on their way to Toys for Less. They each had two dollars and fifty cents to spend at the store's Giant Summer Clearance Sale.

When they reached the store, they saw signs on all the windows:

SUMMER BLOWOUT!
Prices Slashed!
25–50% Off Selected Items

"I hope we find some good stuff," said Max as they went inside. They walked past the first few counters, which displayed the inexpensive toys and prizes like the ones they'd bought for their carnival. They were looking for more expensive, quality items. Max hoped to find something worth five dollars for half off. Then he would have enough money. He didn't have to look far. The idea hit him the moment he saw them.

"That's it!" he cried out. "That's perfect."

"What's it? What's perfect?" asked Gordy.

Max pointed to a box of rubber baseballs. A sign on the box read: 20 CENTS EACH.

"Don't you see? We buy these baseballs for twenty cents each. Then we sell them at a higher price to people who want Dusty Field's autograph."

"You're a genius," said Gordy, slapping Max on

the back. "That's a great idea. All we have to do is figure out how many balls we can buy for our five dollars." He looked up at the ceiling and concentrated. "Let's see now. If each ball costs twenty cents, and we have five dollars. . . . I forget. . . . Do we divide or multiply?"

"We divide," said Max, writing and erasing in the air. "Twenty cents into five dollars . . ."

Gordy was impressed. "How many can we buy, Max?"

"Hold your horses. I have to move the decimals."

Max continued writing, but he stopped suddenly in midair. "Wait. I have another idea. First we have to see the manager."

Max's eyes searched the store for someone who looked like a manager. He saw a young woman walking around, giving orders to the workers.

"That must be the manager," he said, walking toward her.

Gordy followed, and a few minutes later Max was asking, "Excuse me, but are you the manager?"

"Yes," said the young woman. "Can I help you?"

"I was wondering," said Max. "If we buy those rubber baseballs in quantity, how much will you sell them for?"

The manager looked up at the ceiling the way Gordy had done. Max waited nervously.

"How much do you want to spend?" she asked after a while.

"Five dollars—including tax," he answered.

"I'll tell you what. Summer's over. And I need the space more than I need the baseballs. For five dollars—including tax—you can have the whole box. There should be close to fifty balls in there."

"Fifty?" Max cried out. "It's a deal."

"Forty-eight baseballs at fifty cents apiece. We'll really make a fortune, almost," said Max.

"Forty-six," Gordy corrected. "We have to save two for ourselves."

It was Friday morning, and Max and Gordy, each carrying a bag of baseballs, were on their way to the sporting-goods store. It was only nine thirty, and the store didn't open until ten. But they wanted to get there early so they wouldn't miss a single person.

A long line of kids was already forming in front of the store. "Everyone wants to meet Dusty Field," said Max.

"My father said his autograph might become valuable some day," said Gordy. "A real collectible."

Some of the kids had come prepared with base-balls or mitts for autographing. Some had auto-graph books, and a few were holding scraps of paper. But most of them didn't have anything. Max was sure that lots of people would want the baseballs. Well, he was almost sure. He knew he should start selling right away, but he couldn't make himself move. His legs felt like spaghetti. Thinking about selling had been a lot easier than actually doing it. There were so many people. What if nobody wanted to buy any baseballs? What if he and Gordy got chased away by the store owner? Or the police?

Rosalie had warned him about that. She said that he and Gordy needed a license to sell the baseballs. Max didn't know if she knew what she was talking about. He had heard of a dog license. And a license to drive a car. But never a license to sell baseballs.

"What are we waiting for?" asked Gordy.

"You go first," said Max.

"No, you first. It was your idea."

"We'll go together," said Max. He dipped his hand into the bag and pulled out two baseballs. He forced himself to walk along the line of kids and call out, "Baseballs for sale. Just fifty cents." He waved the balls around so everyone could see them. A few people glanced in Max's direction, but turned away.

Gordy, in the meantime, was calling out, "Get your baseballs autographed by Dusty Field. Just fifty cents. Sure to become a collectible."

To his surprise, Max saw that a few kids actually went over to buy some balls from Gordy. Max then took up the call.

"Get your baseballs autographed by Dusty. Just fifty cents. Sure to become valuable." He didn't want to copy Gordy exactly.

A girl with an autograph book came over to buy a ball. "A baseball is better than an autograph book," she said, handing him the money.

A mother with a small boy came by. "I didn't even think to bring anything that Dusty could sign. This is such a good idea."

Some kids with scraps of paper stuffed the papers into their pockets, or dumped them into trash cans. Then they bought baseballs from Max.

Max was having a great time. He could see that Gordy was too. The scene was just as he had pictured. He was selling what people wanted to buy. And the more he sold, the more confident he became. He even began singing "Take Me Out to the Ball Game." The crowd in front of the store joined in.

Suddenly Max stopped singing. Someone inside the store, the manager probably, was standing at the door, staring at Max. Max stared back, and then looked away. This was it! He and Gordy would be asked to leave. He should have known it was too good to last.

The manager opened the door, and the kids pushed their way in. But the manager disappeared. He was nowhere in sight. Neither were the police.

Max decided that if someone came and told him to stop, he would. But until then, he would keep on selling.

He stopped customers before they went into the store. "Get your baseball for Dusty Field's autograph. Fifty cents." Or, "How about a baseball for Dusty's autograph?" Most people were eager to buy.

Dusty was going to be signing autographs until noon. But by eleven, Max and Gordy had sold all their baseballs. All except the two they had saved for themselves.

"I can't believe it," said Max when he and Gordy were waiting in line to meet Dusty. "We sold them all. I thought our goose was cooked when I saw the manager staring at me." Max's mother always used that expression—"my goose was cooked"—even though she had never cooked a goose in her life.

"I can't believe we're getting Dusty's autograph," said Gordy. "I wish the line would move faster. Dusty's hand will get all worn out from shaking hands before he even gets to us."

At last it was Max and Gordy's turn to meet Dusty. Dusty was tall and thin and had a friendly smile. He wasn't wearing a uniform. Just jeans and a T-shirt. But he looked like a ball player anyway.

Max and Dusty shook hands. Dusty said, "Nice to meet you."

But Max couldn't think of anything to say except, "Would you sign this ball to Max?"

"Sure thing," said Dusty, and he signed the ball, *To my pal Max. Dusty Field.*

"Wow! Thanks, Dusty."

Gordy couldn't think of anything great to say either. So he handed Dusty his baseball and said, "I'm Gordy."

Dusty signed, *To my pal Gordy. Dusty Field.*

"Wow!" said Gordy.

"This was a great day," said Max.

"Let's go home and split up the money," said Gordy.

"We made a ton," said Max. "And all because we knew the market. We went where the people were. And we bought in quantity. Just like Austin . . ."

Austin. Max had forgotten all about him. Little Austin Healy, who was home with a scar where his appendix should have been. Austin, who was looking forward to meeting Dusty Field. Why, if it weren't for Austin, Max would never have known about Dusty. He and Gordy would never have bought the balls. They never would've made all that money.

"We can't go home yet," said Max. "There's something we have to do first." He led the way to the baseball section of the store. And there, in a bin, were baseballs. Real league baseballs. They cost three dollars, but Max didn't care. He picked one up and showed it to Gordy.

"For Austin," he said.

"We'll get it autographed by Dusty," said Gordy.

They bought the ball and waited in line again.

"Let's see," said Gordy, looking up at the ceiling. "Not counting what we spent on Austin, if we sold forty-six balls at fifty cents each . . ."

"This time we multiply," said Max.

Max Makes a Million

"**H**ow nice of you to come," said Austin Healy's mother. "Austin will be so happy to see you. He's been feeling a little low today. He had to miss Dusty Field."

"Maybe we can cheer him up," said Max. He thought of the baseball he had for Austin in his bag, and smiled as he went inside.

They found Austin in his room, feeding Newton some freeze-dried shrimp. Austin was wearing sweatpants and a Mickey Mouse sweatshirt.

"Hey, guys. I was thinking about you all day. Did you get to see Dusty?"

"We just came from there," said Max. "How are you feeling?"

"Okay. Do you want to see my scar?"

Max and Gordy shook their heads. "No thanks," said Max.

Austin fed Newton the last of the shrimp and climbed into bed. "I'm supposed to rest up for a few days. And I'm not supposed to laugh. So don't say anything funny. Just tell me about Dusty."

"The place was mobbed," said Max. "Everyone wanted to see him."

"I wanted to see him," said Austin.

"Yeah, that was too bad. Anyway, we got to shake his hand."

"Wow!" said Austin. "I wanted to shake his hand."

"That's rough," said Max.

"And we got his autograph too," Gordy added.

"Wow! That's what I really wanted most. His autograph."

"Really rough," said Max, shaking his head.

"I might never get another chance to meet Dusty," said Austin, looking glum.

"You might not," said Max.

"I might have to wait forever to get his auto-graph." Now Austin was looking even more glum.

"I don't think you'll have to wait that long," Max told him. He turned to Gordy and winked. Then he reached into his bag and took out Austin's baseball.

"From Dusty," he said, handing him the ball.

"For me?" asked Austin, turning the ball around so he could read the autograph. " 'To my pal Austin. Dusty Field.' Oh, boy! This is great. This is the greatest." Austin was so excited, he practically jumped out of bed.

"Watch out for your stitches," said Max.

Austin turned to Max and Gordy and flashed them a smile. The widest smile they had ever seen on Austin's face. "Thanks, guys. Thanks a million."

"A million? Did you hear that, Gordy?" asked Max, slapping him on the back. "We made our million after all."